Disney

Pixar Pals Activities

Parragon

Bath · New York · Singapore · Hong Kong · Cologne · Delhi
Melbourne · Amsterdam · Johannesburg · Shenzhen

ADVENTURE: RACE CAR RUMBLE

Join Lightning McQueen for a new racing adventure. You will meet the Radiator Springs gang, race around the world and have lots of engine-revving fun. Complete the activities to gain your first Pixar friend! You will find even more in the rest of the book.

LIGHTNING AND FRIENDS

Lightning McQueen has lots of friends in Radiator Springs. How many times can you find the word FRIENDS in this wordsearch? Circle the words as you find them.

H	F	A	P	V	Z	A	F
F	R	I	E	N	D	S	R
R	I	G	T	B	Z	P	I
I	E	V	K	O	T	O	E
E	N	O	X	L	O	X	N
N	D	T	B	V	K	B	D
D	S	P	Z	A	A	P	S
S	F	R	I	E	N	D	S

BEST FRIENDS

Lightning's best friend is Mater. They have many adventures together. Use the questions below to write about your best friend.

What is your best friend's name?

What do you like best about your friend?

When is their birthday?

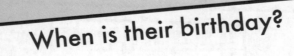

CAR BUDDIES

Draw you and your friend as cars ready for a racing adventure!

What colour will you be?

Will you have a trophy?

What is your racing number?

Lightning and Mater are looking for something fun to do. Help them through the maze so they can go tractor-tippin'.

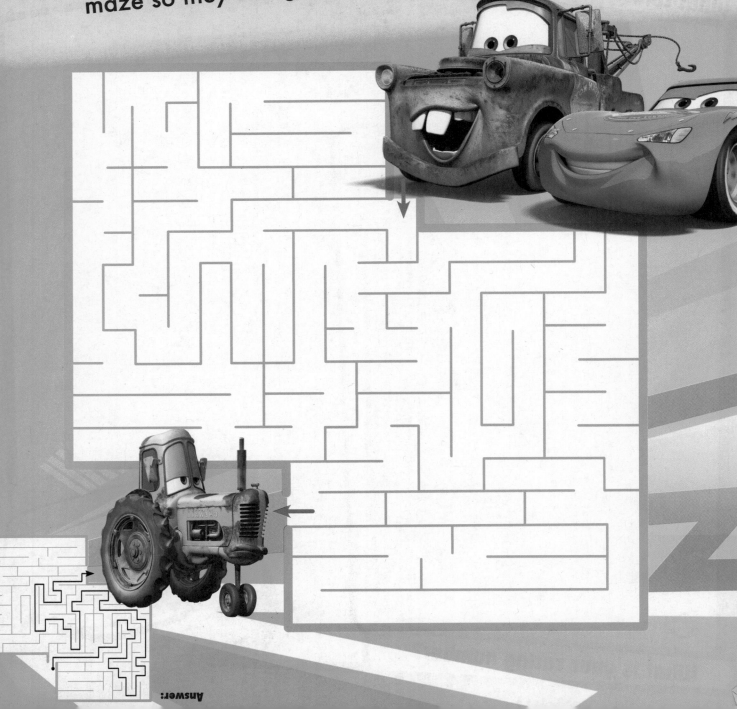

ITALIAN PALS

Luigi and Guido have been friends for years and now work together in Radiator Springs. Can you find five differences between these two pictures of the friends?

WORLD GRAND PRIX

Lightning travels to three different countries on the World Grand Prix. Match the flags to the characters by following the tangled lines.

JAPAN

ITALY

ENGLAND

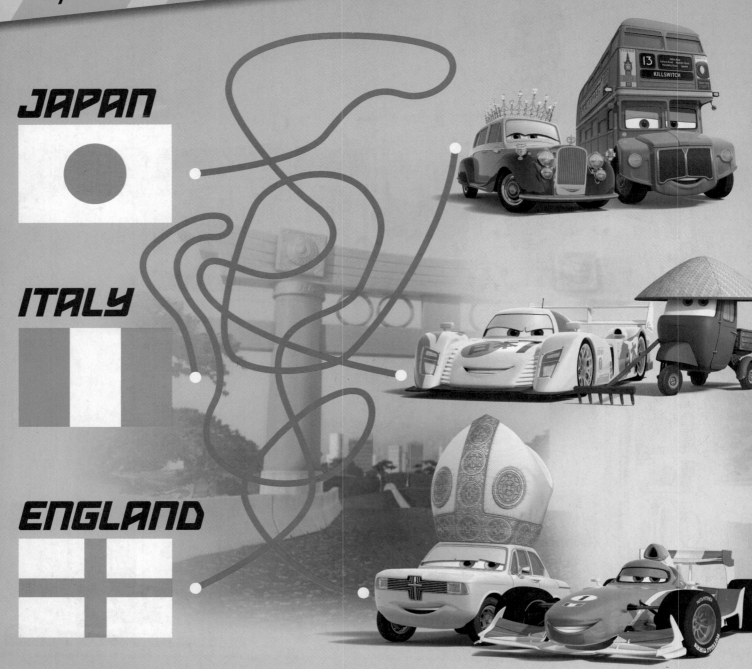

MANY FACES OF MATER

Mater has many silly faces, especially when he is trying new things or having an adventure. One of these faces only appears once on this page – can you find it?

RACE CAR RUMBLE

Well done! You have completed your first adventure. You have gained **Lightning McQueen** as your friend. Colour him in!

Adventure: Toy Box Battle

Are you ready for another adventure? Woody needs your help to save his friends, get back to Andy and play some awesome toy games!

Getting to Know the Toys

Can you name the toy that matches each shadow?
Use the clues to help you.

1. He's got a snake in his boot.

2. He has a laser beam.

3. She's the roughest, toughest cowgirl.

4. "Ride like the wind!"

5. His favourite video game is 'Buzz Lightyear: Attack on Zurg'.

6. Also known as Evil Dr Porkchop (during playtime).

7. He comes with over 30 accessories!

8. He is made out of a spring.

You've Got a Friend in Me

Woody has to get himself and his best friend, Buzz,
back to Andy's house before the big move.
Help them through the maze to Andy's room.

ANDYS
ROOM
KEEP OUT
except MOLLY

Answ

Count the Aliens

Buzz is rounding up the Aliens.
Help him by counting the Aliens on this page.
Write your answer in the box.

Woody's Sheriff Badge

Make some salt dough, then mould yourself a sheriff's badge so you can be just like Woody. Time to round up the bad guys!

... means that you will need an adult to help you.

You will need

Salt dough recipe:
200g plain flour
200g of salt
200ml of water
1 tablespoon of cooking oil

Star-shaped cookie cutter
Baking tray, greased
Gold paint and brush
Sticky badge pin
All-purpose glue

1

Mix the flour and salt in a mixing bowl. Add the water and oil to make the dough.

2

Roll out the dough to about 1cm thick. Cut out some star shapes with the cookie cutter and put them onto a greased baking tray.

3

Make tiny balls with the dough. Wet the points of the stars and stick a ball on each point. Leave them to dry for three days. Paint them gold and leave to dry. Glue a sticky badge pin to the back of each star.

SHERIFF WOODY's Game idea:

Get three or more friends together. One player is Sheriff Woody and wears the badge. The other players hide — they are villains on the run! Once found, a player becomes the sheriff, wears the badge and helps look for all the others!

Toy Rescue

Buzz needs to save Woody after Al takes him to his Toy Barn. Can you find which path Buzz must take to reach Woody?

A

C

B

Escape from Sunnyside

Read the story aloud and replace the pictures with the words that match.

 **Andy**

 **Woody**

 **Lotso**

 **Buzz**

 Toys

 was going to college and he planned to leave his behind in the attic. His mum mistook them for rubbish so put them out for the bin men. Luckily and the rest of the escaped to Sunnyside Daycare Centre. There they met , a mean old bear who made and his friends play with the rough younger children. arrived to stop and help the get back to 's house safe and sound. Phew! What an adventure.

Toy Box Battle

Congratulations! You've completed another adventure. You have gained **Woody** as your friend. Colour him in now.

ADVENTURE: MONSTER MADNESS

Your next adventure is with Sulley, Mike and all their monster friends. Let's get Boo back home, save Monsters, Inc. and have a roaring good time!

WHERE'S BOO?

When Boo, the human girl, ends up in Monstropolis, Sulley and Mike must get her home! Can you help them find the real Boo? *Hint: She is different from all the othe*

MONSTER MATES

This is Mike and Sulley's greatest adventure yet. Can you draw these two best friends using the grid as a guide?

MISCHIEF MAKER

One of the scarers at Monsters, Inc. is up to no good. How many times can you find the word RANDALL in this wordsearch?

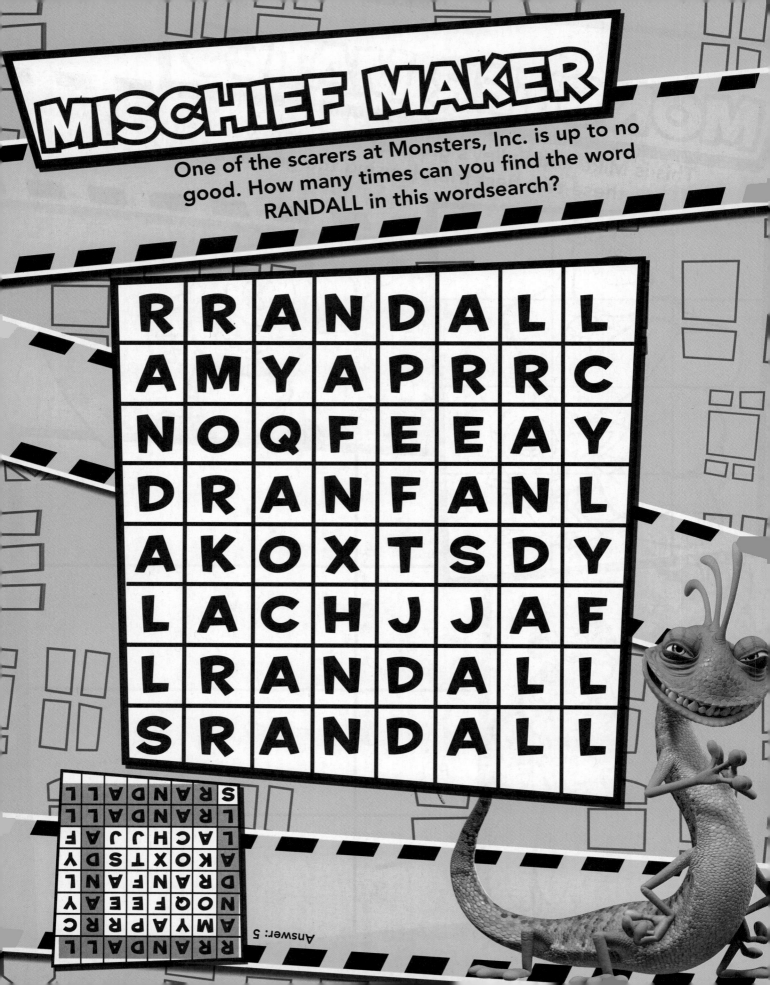

R	R	A	N	D	A	L	L
A	M	Y	A	P	R	R	C
N	O	Q	F	E	E	A	Y
D	R	A	N	F	A	N	L
A	K	O	X	T	S	D	Y
L	A	C	H	J	J	A	F
L	R	A	N	D	A	L	L
S	R	A	N	D	A	L	L

Answer: 5

RANDALL BOGGS

Well done, you have found the troublemaker. Copy the colours to complete this picture of Randall.

MY MONSTER

Ever wondered what it would be like to be a monster? Circle the words that you would pick to describe yourself if you were a monster.

HAIRY

SMALL

SCALY

SCARY

SHY

BIG

EYES: 1 2 3 4

PANIC STATION!

Sulley, Mike and Boo are on the run from Randall. Can you spot five differences between these two pictures?

Answers:

RACE TO BOO'S

Time to get Boo home. Help Mike and Sulley get through the maze to Boo's door. Watch out for Randall!

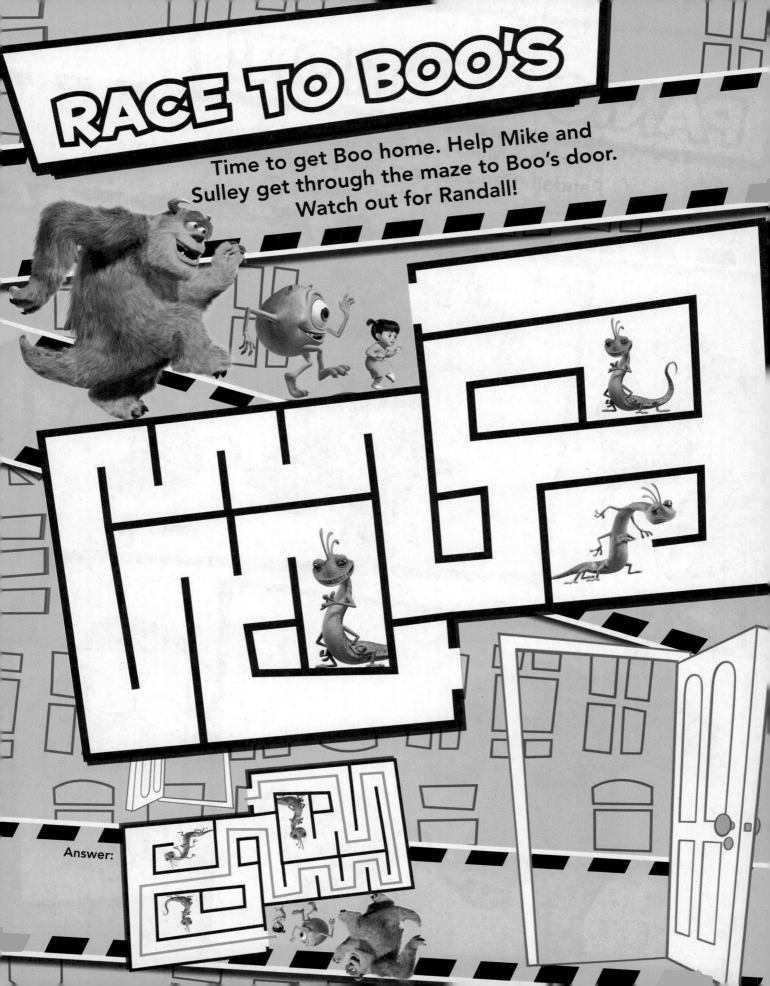

Answer:

LAUGH FLOOR

Now that Sulley has worked out that laughs provide more power than screams he wants funny monsters, not scary ones! How many of Mike's best jokes are here?

Q: WHAT'S THE DIFFERENCE BETWEEN A FISH AND A PIANO?
A: YOU CAN TUNE A PIANO, BUT YOU CAN'T TUNA FISH!

Q: WHAT DO YOU CALL A FLY WITH NO WINGS?
A: A WALK!

Q: WHY DID THE CYCLOPS STOP TEACHING?
A: BECAUSE HE ONLY HAD ONE PUPIL.

Q: WHAT IS A SEA MONSTER'S FAVOURITE MEAL?
A: FISH AND SHIPS!

Q: WHAT'S BIG, SCARY AND HAS TWO WHEELS?
A: A MONSTER ON A MOTORBIKE!

YOUR ANSWER

....

Answer: 5

MONSTER MADNESS

Phew! That was a tough one! You have finished the adventure and gained Mike as a friend. Colour him in!

Adventure: Ocean Outing

Time for some underwater fun with Marlin and Nemo. Complete the games and puzzles and find your new fishy friend!

Fancy Fish

Nemo and his dad live under the sea, where there are many different types of fish. Make some of your own, then hang them up in the window and see them shine!

1

Fold a piece of card 40 x 30cm in half. Draw half a fish shape then cut it out.

You will need:

- Card (cut from a cereal box)
- Pencil
- Scissors
- Kitchen foil
- Coloured sweet wrappers and foil
- Glue
- Brush
- White card
- Felt-tip pens
- Thread and tape to hang up

2

Place the template onto card and draw around the edge. Cut it out. You can use the template again and again.

3

Cut two pieces of foil roughly the same size as the fish. Crinkle the foil a bit then glue both pieces to the card fish. Trim around the edges.

4

Glue coloured wrappers/foil onto both sides to make patterns. Glue a white card circle onto both sides for eyes. Make a black dot with a felt-tip pen. Tape thread to the top of the fish then hang it up.

Nemo's tip:
It's fun to make these fish with a best friend and make one for each other!

... means that you will need an adult to help you.

Finding Nemo

The ocean is a crowded place. Can you find
Nemo amongst all these other sea creatures?

Answer:

Homeward Bound

Marlin and Nemo are heading home. Help them through the maze back to the drop off.

Start

Finish

Answer:

Ocean Outing

You've made a splash! For completing this adventure, you gain Nemo as a Pixar Friend. Colour him and his dad in bright orange.

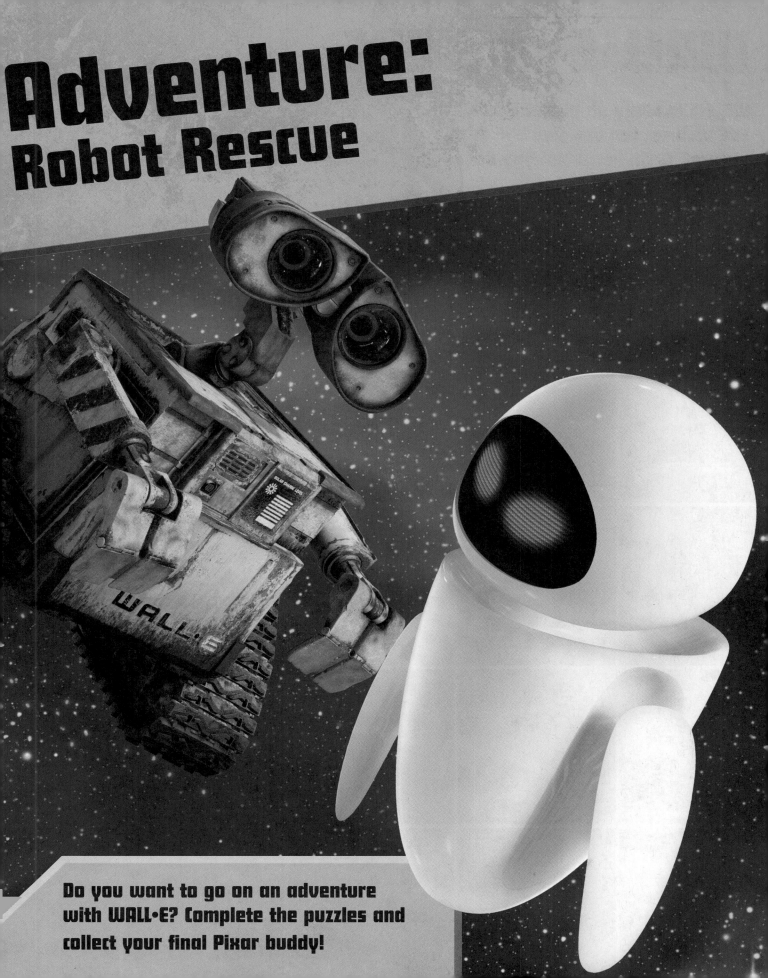

Adventure:
Robot Rescue

Do you want to go on an adventure
with WALL·E? Complete the puzzles and
collect your final Pixar buddy!

WALL•E and EVE

WALL•E is alone on planet Earth until EVE arrives. Can you find EVE in this picture? Circle her when you do.

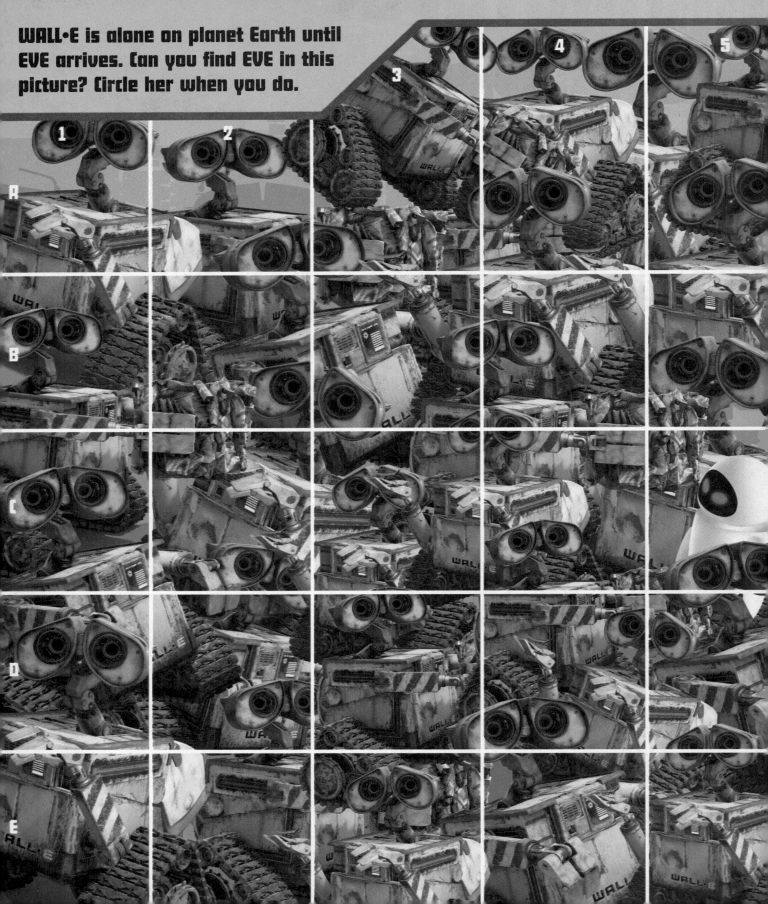

Create a Robot

WALL·E and EVE are robots from different worlds. Can you draw your own robot here? Will it be from outer space like EVE?

How big will it be?

What colour will it be?

What special gadget will it have?

WALL·E's Treasure

WALL·E loves to collect things from planet Earth. Look at the patterns below and choose the object that should go next. Write the correct letter using the pictures at the top of the page.

Earth Adventure

WALL·E and EVE need to get back to Earth to save the day. Can you help them find which path will take them home?

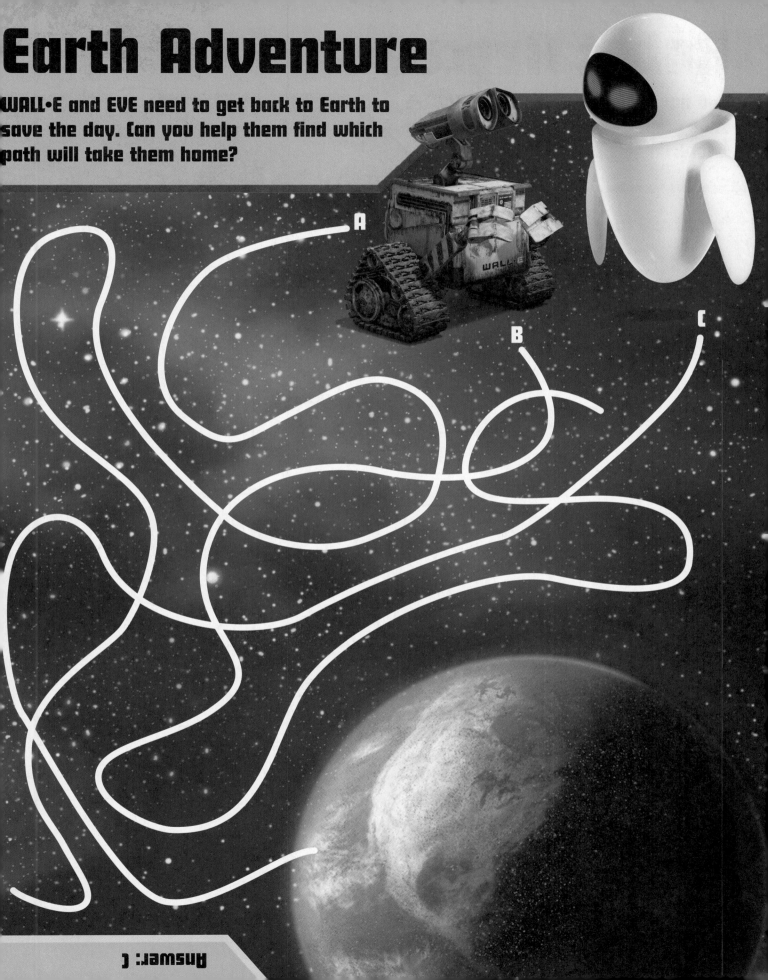

A

B

C

Robot Rescue

You have done it! You helped WALL•E save planet Earth and now he's your final friend! Colour him in!

Adventure: Pixar Pals

All your friends are here! Draw a line to match each character to their friends.

1

A

2

B

3

C

4

D

5

E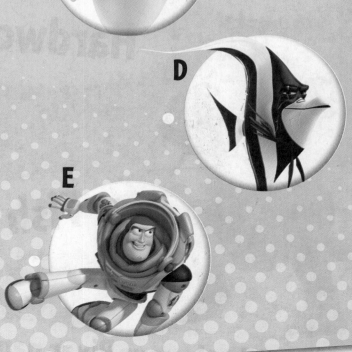

Pixar Picks

Would you like to join the world of Pixar? What would your character be like? Circle the words that you think would describe your character.

Scary

Adventurer

Monster

Fun

Hero

Toy

Robot

Funny

Hardworking

Serious

Car

Fish

What's your Pixar name? . . . .

My Pixar Character

Now you know what your Pixar character is like draw it here.

Copy Colouring

The Pixar gang thank you for your help on their missions.
Look at the colours of each character and try to copy them!

Well done! Colour in your pals and complete the certificate.

Pixar Pal

Congratulations!

....

has completed his/her adventures and is now a Pixar Pal.